TO

CALUM

HAVE A LOVELY XMAS
2004.

ALL OUR LOVE

MUMMY + DADDY.

X   X   X   X   X

THE LITTLE RED TRAIN STORYBOOK

This edition produced for The Book People Ltd,
Hall Wood Avenue, Haydock, St Helens, WA11 9UL

The Runaway Train first published by Julia MacRae in 1995
Little Red Train to the Rescue first published by Julia MacRae in 1997
Faster, Faster, Little Red Train first published by Julia MacRae in 1999
Green Light for the Little Red Train first published by Hutchinson in 2002

This Book People edition published 2004

1 3 5 7 9 10 8 6 4 2

RANDOM HOUSE CHILDREN'S BOOKS
61–63 Uxbridge Road, London W5 5SA
A division of The Random House Group Ltd

RANDOM HOUSE AUSTRALIA (PTY) LTD
20 Alfred Street, Milsons Point, Sydney,
New South Wales 2061, Australia

RANDOM HOUSE NEW ZEALAND LTD
18 Poland Road, Glenfield, Auckland 10, New Zealand

RANDOM HOUSE (PTY) LTD
Endulini, 5A Jubilee Road, Parktown 2193, South Africa

THE RANDOM HOUSE GROUP Limited Reg. No. 954009

A CIP catalogue record for this book is available from the British Library.

Printed in Singapore

THE LITTLE RED TRAIN
STORYBOOK

Four Fabulous Adventures

Benedict Blathwayt

TED SMART

THE RUNAWAY TRAIN

Duffy Driver overslept.
Everyone was waiting at the
station for the little red train.

When Duffy was ready to start, he saw an old lady running down the platform. "I'll help you," he said. But he forgot to put the brake on and the little red train set off down the track . . . *Chuff-chuff, chuff-chuff, whoo . . . oooo*

Duffy saw a lorry. "Stop!" Duffy shouted. "I must catch up with the runaway train!"

"Jump in," cried the lorry driver and off they went after the little red train . . . *Chuff-chuff, chuff-chuff, whoo . . . oooo . . .*

. . . until they came to a traffic jam.

Duffy saw a boat. "Ahoy there!" Duffy shouted. "I must catch
up with the runaway train!"
"All aboard," cried the boatman and off they all went after the
little red train . . . *Chuff-chuff, chuff-chuff, whoo . . . oooo . . .*

. . . until the river turned away from the railway.

Duffy saw some bicycles. "Help!" Duffy shouted. "I must catch up with the runaway train!"

"Jump on," cried the cyclists and off they all went after the little red train . . . *Chuff-chuff, chuff-chuff, whoo . . . oooo . . .*

. . . until they ran into a flock of sheep.

Duffy saw some ponies. "Whoa!" Duffy shouted. "I must catch up with the runaway train!"
"Up you come," cried the riders and off they all went after the little red train . . . *Chuff-chuff, chuff-chuff, whoo . . . oooo . . .*

. . . until the ponies could go no further.

Duffy saw a tractor. "Halloo!" Duffy shouted. "I must catch up
with the runaway train!"
"Get on then," cried the farmer and off they went after the little
red train . . . *Chuff-chuff, chuff-chuff, whoo . . . oooo . . .*

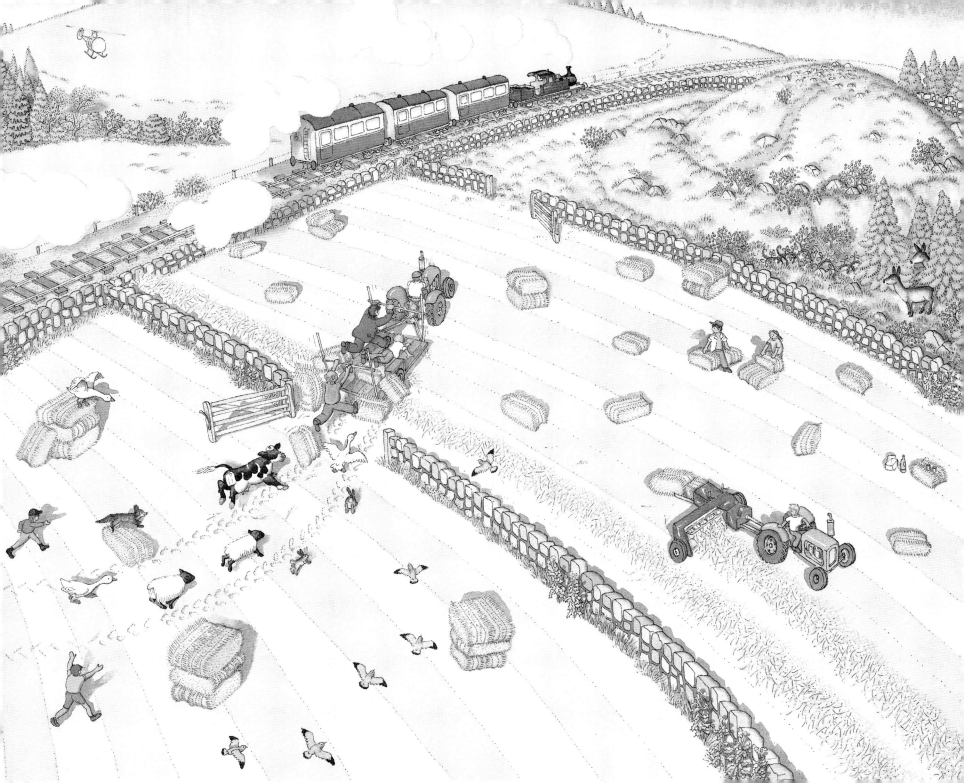

. . . until they were spotted by a helicopter pilot.

"My last chance!" gasped Duffy. "I must catch up with the runaway train!"

"Climb in quick," said the pilot and Duffy climbed in, while the lorry driver, the boatman, the cyclists, the riders and the farmer all stood and watched . . .

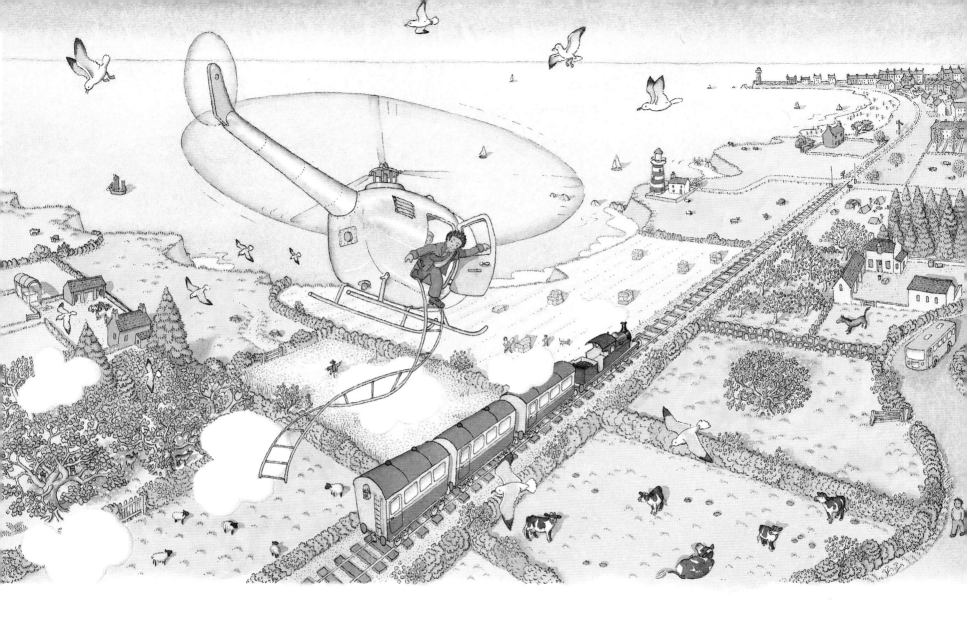

as Duffy caught up with the runaway train . . . *Chuff-chuff,*
chuffitty-chuff, whoo . . . oo . . . oo

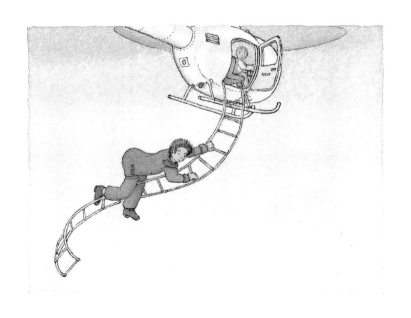

And Duffy Driver drove the little red train into the station at Sandy-on-Sea and spent a lovely lazy afternoon on the beach before he had to drive back home again.

Chuff-chuff, chuffitty -chuff, whoo . . . eee . . . eee . . .

LITTLE RED TRAIN
TO THE RESCUE

One wet and windy day, Duffy
Driver lit the fire in the little red
train and collected three trucks
from the goods yard.

The trucks were soon loaded and Duffy Driver and the little
red train set off for Birchcombe village, high up in the hills.
Chuff-chuff,chuffitty-chuff...

But as they came round a bend, what did they see...

Animals on the line!
Duffy put on the brakes with a scree...eee...ch
and the little red train stopped just in time.

When the animals were back in the
farmyard, the little red train set off again.
Chuff-chuff, chuffitty-chuff...

But as they came round a bend, what did they see...

The river had flooded the road!
Duffy put on the brakes with a scree...eee...ch
and the little red train stopped just in time.

They rescued the passengers from the bus on
the bridge and the little red train set off again.
Chuff-chuff, chuffitty-chuff...
But as they came round a bend, what did they see...

The wind had blown down a tree!
Duffy put on the brakes with a scree...eee...ch
and the little red train stopped just in time.

Everyone helped to move the tree
and the little red train set off again.
Chuff-chuff, chuffitty-chuff...

But the track got steeper and steeper and
the little red train hotter and hotter until...

P O P! HISSSSS! The safety valve blew off the boiler!
Duffy Driver put on the brakes with a scree...eee...ch
and stopped to let the little red train cool down.

Up in the hills there was snow,
so they set off again more slowly.
Chuff-chuff-chuff, chuu...ff, chuff...itty-chu...ff...
But as they came round a bend, what did they see...

A great pile of snow was blocking the line!
Duffy put on the brakes with a scree...eee...ch
and the little red train stopped just in time.

They all helped to clear the snow
and the little red train set off again.
Chuff-chuff, chuffitty-chuff...

But as they came to the last stretch
of line what did they find...

The points had frozen!
The little red train went off the wrong way.
Duffy put on the brakes with a scree...eee...ch
and the little red train stopped just in time.

The signalman poured hot water on
the points and with a chuff-chuff,
chuffitty-chuff the little red train ran
on towards the station at Birchcombe...

POST OFFICE

Everyone was there to greet them.
Duffy Driver blew the whistle, whee...eee...eee
and put on the brakes with a scree...eee...ch and the
little red train stopped at the platform just in time.

The passengers climbed down and helped to unload the supplies...

and Duffy Driver was given a special tea by the postmistress.

Then Duffy got back into the driver's
cab and after he had blown the whistle,
whee...eee...eee, the little red train raced
back home. It was downhill all the way.

Chuffitty-chuffitty,
chuffitty-chuff...

FASTER, FASTER, LITTLE RED TRAIN

Duffy Driver was eating his
breakfast when the telephone rang.
"The fast train to Pebblecombe has
broken down," he said. "The Little
Red Train is needed. I'll have to rush."

The passengers from the broken-down train were
cross and worried. "Will the Little Red Train get
there on time, we don't want to miss the fair!"
"All aboard for Pebblecombe," called Duffy Driver.
"We'll go as fast as we can!"
Chuff chuff went the Little Red Train.
Click clack went the wheels on the track.

Their first stop was Newtown.

"Who's for Pebblecombe fair?" shouted Duffy Driver.

"Quick as you can!"

A lady with a big box of strawberries climbed on board.

Whoosh went the steam from the Little Red Train.

Click clack went the wheels on the track.

Click clack clicketty clack.

Next they stopped at Woodhaven.

"Jump on for Pebblecombe fair!" shouted Duffy Driver.

A man with a crate of hens squeezed into the carriage.

"You're running late," he grumbled.

"We're doing our best," Duffy Driver said cheerfully.

Chuff chuff went the Little Red Train.

Click clack went the wheels on the track.

Click clack clicketty clack.

The Little Red Train stopped at Castle Down.
"We're in a hurry," said Duffy Driver, "this train's
for Pebblecombe fair."
A gang of noisy children climbed on board.
Chuff chuff went the Little Red Train.
Chuff chuff, chuffitty chuff...

The next station was Old Harbour.

"Any passengers for Pebblecombe?" called Duffy Driver.

"Is this the right train?" said a boy with a great big dog.

"It is the right train," said Duffy. "And we've no time to lose."

Whoo…eee… whistled the Little Red Train.

Chuff chuff chuffitty chuff.

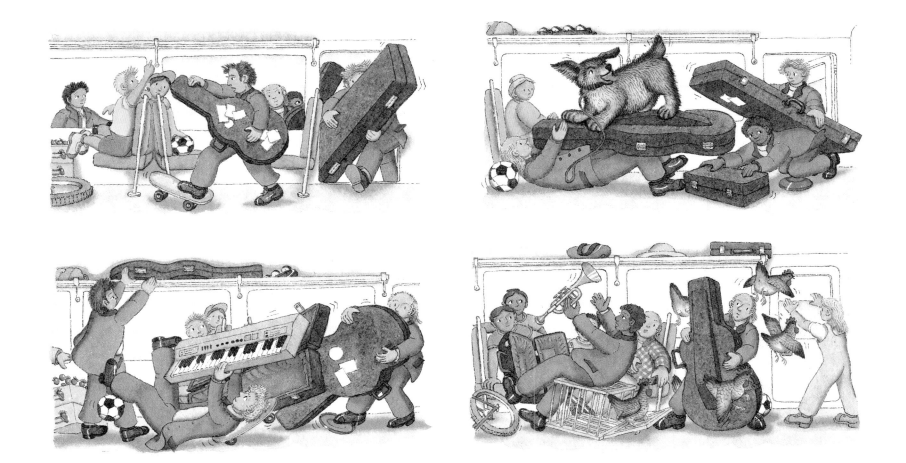

When they stopped at Hillside station, there were four musicians
waiting on the platform.

"We're playing at Pebblecombe fair," they grumbled,

"and we're going to be late."

"In you get," said Duffy briskly, "we're going as fast as we can."

Whoo...eee... went the Little Red Train. *Whoo...eeee...*

The Little Red Train went faster than ever before.

Click clack went the wheels on the track.

Clicketty clicketty clicketty clack.

"Slow down," said the lady with the strawberries.

"Slow down!" shouted the man with the crate of hens.

"Slow down!" shrieked the boy with the great big dog.

"Steady on!" cried the musicians.

"Faster ... faster!" yelled the noisy children.

But Duffy Driver couldn't hear anyone shouting.
He shovelled more coal into the firebox and
the boiler made more and more steam and
the wheels of the Little Red Train went
faster and faster and faster...
Clicketty clicketty clicketty clicketty clicketty clicketty clack.

And right on time the Little Red Train
pulled into the station at Pebblecombe.

Out got the lady with her box of strawberries, the man with the hens and the boy with the dog and the four musicians and the gang of noisy children.

They thanked Duffy Driver and the
Little Red Train for getting them to
Pebblecombe so fast. Then they all
went off to spend the day at the fair.

Duffy Driver thought he would have another breakfast.
"You're the Little Red Express now," he said as he wiped
down the fenders.

*Whoo…eeee…*went the Little Red Train.

Whoo…oooo…eeee…

GREEN LIGHT FOR
THE LITTLE RED TRAIN

Duffy Driver and the Little Red Train arrived at the station to pick up their passengers.

"There's repair work further up the line," said Jack the guard. "You'll be following a different route today. Keep going as long as the lights are green."

"Right," said Duffy.

Sure enough, the points on the railway tracks sent Duffy one way and then another.

The line carried them down into a dark tunnel.

Duffy didn't realize they were under the sea!

When they came out at the other end, the signal shone green so Duffy and the Little Red Train kept going.

Duffy didn't realize he was in France. Shouldn't I be back on my usual tracks by now? he thought.

When they reached the next station, Duffy slowed down to ask what was going on.

But a noisy electric train clanked up behind them.
PEEP . . . PEEP . . . PEEP, it whistled.
  "Oh, go blow a fuse!" grumbled Duffy, and the
Little Red Train picked up speed again.

Duffy had no idea that he was now in Spain.
But the lights were still green so the Little Red
Train flew along at a tremendous rate.
    Clicketty clicketty clicketty clack

They went so fast and the sun was so hot that the Little Red Train's water tanks ran dry and the needle on the pressure gauge pointed to DANGER.

"Water!" shouted Duffy, putting on the brake. "We need water or the train will explode!"

Luckily there was water just ahead.
Everyone jumped down and helped
to fill the Little Red Train's water tanks.
TOOT . . . TOOT . . . TOOT, tooted
an impatient freight train behind them.
"Oh, nuts and bolts to you!" hissed Duffy.
But the signal far down the line shone
green so off they had to go again.

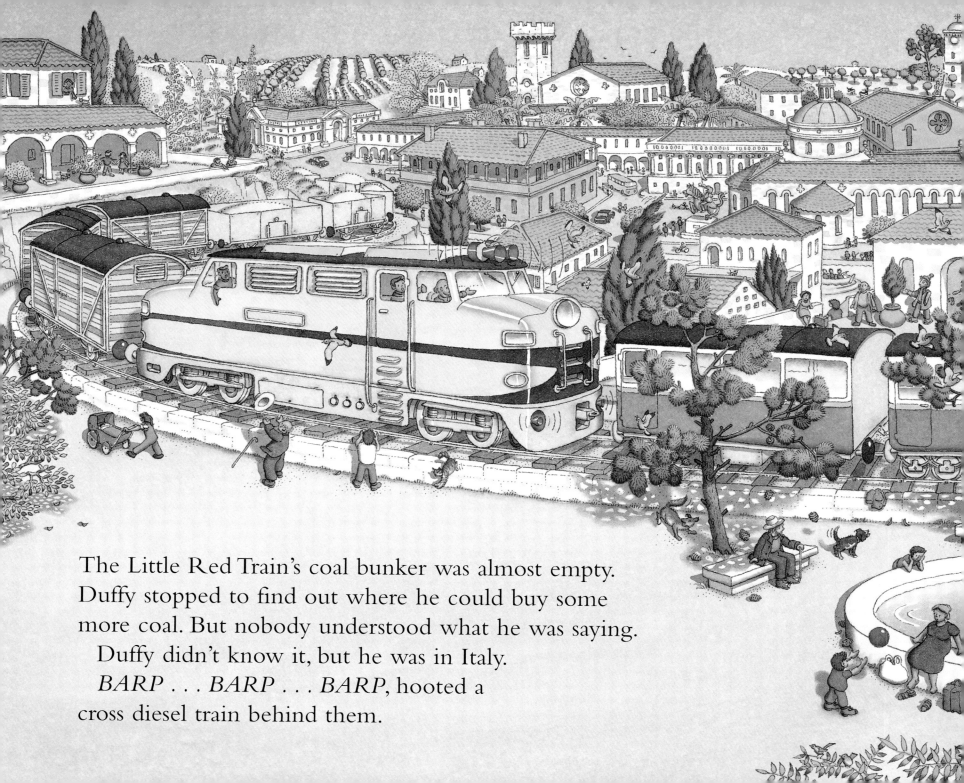

The Little Red Train's coal bunker was almost empty. Duffy stopped to find out where he could buy some more coal. But nobody understood what he was saying.

Duffy didn't know it, but he was in Italy.

BARP . . . BARP . . . BARP, hooted a cross diesel train behind them.

"Oh, go pop your rivets!" shouted Duffy.

But the signal lights glowed green so Duffy blew the whistle and let off the brake and they were soon speeding along again at a sizzling pace.

Whoo . . . ooo . . . eee

Chuffitty chuffitty chuffitty chuff

When the last lump of coal was gone, the fire in the firebox went out and the Little Red Train stopped.

"We're stuck!" cried Duffy.

So everyone jumped down and gathered dry wood until the Little Red Train's coal bunker was full.

But . . .

. . . *HOO* . . . *HOO* . . . *HOO*, honked a furious express train behind them.

"Oh, smoke and smuts to you!" yelled Duffy.

He lit a new fire in the firebox and soon the Little Red Train had built up enough steam to get going again.

This is the longest detour I've ever had to take,
thought Duffy. But he had no idea just how far
north he had come. He opened the throttle
as wide as it would go and the Little Red Train's
wheels spun and the wind whistled past until . . .

. . . a signal ahead shone RED!

Duffy heaved on the brake and the wheels locked and the Little Red Train slid along in a shower of sparks and stopped just an inch away from the end of the line.

Duffy was so tired that he didn't realize he was on a ferry. He knew he had done his best and obeyed signals when they were green and stopped when they were red – so he settled down in his cab for a well-earned snooze.

Duffy woke with a jolt when the ferry docked. He
was told by a rather cross man to get going.

The Little Red Train sped through the night and
the signals shone green all the way.

"Where have you been?" asked Jack the guard when they arrived back at the station.

Duffy shrugged his shoulders. "Your guess is as good as mine," he said, "but it's really good to be home."

The Little Red Train let out a great sigh of steam.

Whoo . . . eee . . . whoo . . . eee . . . eee . . .